T0294311

More Praise for
Animal Children

Animal Children is a book of tender, surreal masculinity, full of nurturing alchemists, cities moaning because they wish to be wild, and the very best kissers. Reminiscent of Charlie Simic and Kenji Miyazawa, Behm-Steinberg understands the gentle twist that can make a piece come alive, like a balloon animist who squeak squeak squeaks something seemingly simple into sudden delight. "I talk to you about love, I do it every day. I'd do it even if nothing green grew inside me. I'd do it even if nobody paid me for anything," Behm-Steinberg writes. *Animal Children* teems with rare, quiet, radical hope: read it and feel heartened.

— **KATIE FARRIS**, author of *boysgirls*

The world is always in wonder in *Animal Children*, Hugh Behm-Steinberg's garden of surreal delights, a fecund plot of deadpan fantasies with a tender heart in love. Everything is possible here according to the permissive rules of language and uniquely conceived idiom. What Behm-Steinberg recognizes so essentially is how choice makes a paradise of hell, how a world where anything goes can be an anarchy, too, of comity, as we only have to wish.

— **MICHAEL MEJIA**, author of *TOKYO*

"At the reading, everyone falls asleep," begins the first brief story in Hugh Behm-Steinberg's *Animal Children*. We readers become that audience, somnambulating our way through generously domestic dreamscapes in which God creates the universe to keep boredom-prone Death busy and in which there's a store where you can shop for your third eye. Alchemist to zombie cure, these flash pieces will lovingly muck up anyone's sluggish relationship to the everyday.

— **PAULA CISEWSKI**, author of *Quitter*

Hugh Behm-Steinberg's sentences are crisp, uncluttered and mercifully free of pretense. They are also enviously imaginative, immediately satisfying and entirely musical. If you need a break (and I know I do) from predictable story arcs and their accompanying monotony, waste not a moment longer and go get yourself a copy of *Animal Children*. Hugh's is one of the most distinct, original, and inspiring voices in contemporary literature, a worthy heir to the likes of Russell Edson and James Tate.

– **PETER BULLEN**, author of *Wallflower*

A striking menagerie of the whimsical and surreal that will writhe around your sense of reality. From cows learning Kung Fu to eels who won't leave your body, the brief (and often wild) encounters in *Animal Children* had me both laughing and scratching at my skin. An achievement in miniatures in the vein of Etgar Keret from one of our funniest and most inventive writers.

– **SEQUOIA NAGAMATSU**, author of
Where We Go When All We Were Is Gone

Animal Children

Hugh Behm-Steinberg

NOMADIC
PRESS

OAKLAND

111 FAIRMOUNT AVENUE
OAKLAND, CA 94611

BROOKLYN

475 KENT AVENUE #302
BROOKLYN, NY 11249

WWW.NOMADICPRESS.ORG

MASTHEAD

FOUNDING AND MANAGING EDITOR
J. K. FOWLER

ASSOCIATE EDITOR
MICHAELA MULLIN

DESIGN
J. K. FOWLER

MISSION STATEMENT

Nomadic Press is a 501 (C)(3) not-for-profit organization that supports the works of emerging and established writers and artists. Through publications (including translations) and performances, Nomadic Press aims to build community among artists and across disciplines.

SUBMISSIONS

Nomadic Press wholeheartedly accepts unsolicited book manuscripts. To submit your work, please visit www.nomadicpress.org/submissions

DISTRIBUTION

Orders by trade bookstores and wholesalers:
Small Press Distribution,
1341 Seventh Street
Berkeley, CA 94701
spd@spdbooks.org
(510) 524-1668 / (800) 869-7553

Animal Children

© 2020 by Hugh Behm-Steinberg

This book was made possible by a loving community of chosen family and friends, old and new.

For author questions or to book a reading at your bookstore, university/school, or alternative establishment, please send an email to info@nomadicpress.org.

Cover artwork and author portrait by Arthur Johnstone

Published by Nomadic Press, 111 Fairmount Avenue, Oakland, CA 94611

First printing, 2020

Printed in the United States of America

LIBRARY OF CONGRESS CATALOGING-IN-PUBLICATION DATA

Behm-Steinberg, Hugh 1968 –
Title: *Animal Children*
P. CM.
Summary: The brief narratives in *Animal Children* by Hugh Behm-Steinberg work like a deceptively simple pinhole camera, a way of gazing at the deepest secrets of the heart through a lens of surrealism, humor, and pathos that renders clear that which is too intense, too personal, or too profound to be directly gazed upon. From the inner workings of 4-H clubs raising prize-winning nuns to the trials and tribulations of dating (and breaking up with) Death and Nature, to the insistence of cattle demanding to learn Kung Fu and people falling asleep during poetry readings, you will leave this book cleansed of your illusions, dazzled by hypnotic story-telling, and filled with a sense of wonder that lasts and lasts.

[1. POETRY/PROSE POEMS. 3. FICTION/MICROFICTIONS. 3. AMERICAN GENERAL.] I. III. TITLE.

LIBRARY OF CONGRESS CONTROL NUMBER: 2019957644

ISBN: 978-1-7327866-5-3

Animal
Children

Hugh Behm-Steinberg

**NOMADIC
PRESS**

for Mary

CONTENTS

INTRODUCTION

In 2015, I had just completed a chapbook of weird little prose pieces about *The Sound of Music*—things like imagining if HP Lovecraft had written the musical, or what happened to the Von Trapp mansion after they had abandoned it, or how my teachers would screen that movie in biology class and how miserable it made me feel. I thought, "Great! I'll just pick a couple more movies, write poems about them, and that'll be my next book!" So I started writing poems about movies, but all of them were terrible. It turned out that what was calling to me was the idea of writing weird little narratives.

As a poet, I've always resisted straight-ahead narratives. I like my poems to leap, to not be essays or stories but something more mysterious, harder to figure out. But as one of my teachers told me, "that which you resist is what's calling you."

So why not try telling stories? What's great about fiction is that it's fiction: you're free to make stuff up, you're free to make those leaps, you're free to do all sorts of poety stuff, but you also get to have such cool things as conflicts, plots, characters, worlds. There's room in all those extra words to observe and describe. You get to be other people, and you get to put words in the mouths of all sorts beings, human and others. And something alchemical happens when you're quick about it.

THE SEA

At the reading everyone falls asleep.

The reader, initially dismayed, forges ahead anyway. If not awake, then in dreams, maybe something will stick.

The audience snaps awake. "Were we snoring?" they ask.

The reader says, "Yes, but that's okay," and goes back to reading. The audience shifts uncomfortably in their chairs, trying to stay awake. Discreetly they pinch themselves, they bite their lips, they poke their neighbors. All attempts fail, down they all go, everyone back to sleep.

It sounds like the ocean, so the reader skips ahead and reads the part about the fish.

GOODWILL

I die and have to go back to retrieve my birth clothes. They're in a pile, warm, like they just came out of the drier. I fold them carefully, awestruck by how small I used to be. I put them in a wicker basket, which I hoist onto my shoulder because I have to walk a very long way, to the only Goodwill store for miles around.

The store is calm in its solitude, like a horse sleeping, surrounded by fields and lawns, trees, parkland and wilderness, gardens. I go inside and there's all these people shopping, clothes of all sorts hang from racks, books, cups and dish sets, some brown furniture, nothing remarkable, the same things you'd find at a Goodwill anywhere else.

I go to the back with my birth clothes; I hand them to the lady, so grateful I don't have to sell them. They're still warm. The lady smiles at me, as she examines each piece for tears. "Look at this," she says as she shows me the collar of a tiny undershirt, so worn and soft it's almost transparent, a little blank label.

"There's room there for you to write something," she says, "for the next person who's going to wear your clothes."

There's so much I want to say, and there's so little room in which to say it. My hands are trembling so much I keep dropping the pen.

"That's ok," the lady says, and she writes what she always writes, in letters too small for anyone to read.

THE CATTLE

One day, a herd of cattle appeared at the gates of the Shaolin Temple, and they would not stop lowing, nor would they let anyone drive them away. So the abbot, who was sufficiently wise he could understand the language of animals, was sent for, and when he arrived one of the cows said, "There is so much suffering and injustice in the world; it is worse for cattle. We demand that you teach us Kung Fu!"

"But you are cattle," the abbot said. "Kung Fu is for the people."

The cattle were furious to hear this. "How can you say there is justice for some and not for the rest of us? Are we only born into this world to pull your plows, to feed you with the meat of our bodies and the milk meant for our children? Your shoes are made from our skin, and your books are held together with glue made from our bones. We are stabbed with spears and strangled with ropes for your entertainment. Teach us Kung Fu or Kung Fu is meaninglessness, for knowledge without justice is the most barren desert there is!"

Their logic was persuasive. It was clear the cattle would gladly endure any hardship, so rapidly they learned all the steps and poses: tiger and leopard, snake and crane. Effortlessly they mastered dragon style, where any part of the body is a target; finally, knowing all that could be learned each of them chose to become teachers, leaving the Temple as suddenly as they arrived.

"Justice, justice, justice!" they lowed; the ground quaked and the dust they kicked up hid the sky.

"You have made a terrible mistake," said the Abbot's rooster.

"That depends on whether they get what they want," replied the Abbot.

GENTLENESS

I was such a tough kid all the cattle would stop by our house to chew on me. They'd ring the doorbell, or they'd wait for me as I was walking home from school. Their hot breath, their sad eyes as my salt taste filled their mouths.

My mother, unlike all the other mothers, watched. I didn't complain, but neither did my brothers or sisters, who I had beaten up mercilessly. "Serves you right," each of them said, when they weren't busy petting the cows. So each day the cattle chewed and chewed, but in their mouths I stayed whole.

It took such a long time to become gentle.

SOFT SPOT

When you're no longer a baby, after you start wearing grownup clothes and big person shoes, after you outgrow the safety seat and you start driving your mom around instead, you ask, "Why can't I be a baby? I'd be a very good baby. This time I'd get it right, being a baby."

You drive past the Toys "R" Us, you drive past the great fountain of money and you drive around the mortuary.

"No matter how good you've been you're not getting anything," your mom tells you from the backseat, "because you're a grownup now. Grownups never get anything just because they've been good."

"Beg all you want," she says. "I'm never giving you your soft spot back."

5

4-H

My son's hobby is raising nuns; he keeps them in the barn behind our house. He lets them loose in the field each day for exercise; they forage quietly and grow shiny and plump. When the 4-H Fair comes to town, he'll show them off along with all the other nuns raised by the rest of the kids in the county. The judges will be strict, as they examine each nun and make notes on their clipboards, but my son is nonplussed. He will be praised for the quality of their headaches and the curliness of their tails. "That's a fine blue-ribboned nun you got there," they'll all say. Some of the nuns he'll sell, some he'll keep, the rest he sets free, where they wander among the poor, blinking rapidly as they stare up at the sky.

ME AND MY OWL

I wait in the office, me and my owl. I'm writing in my notebook: characters, backgrounds, plot points and world building, but nothing makes sense.

"You need to eat more mice," my owl says.

"Three each day. Isn't that enough?" I ask, grinding my teeth. They taste horrible so I swallow them whole.

"Not if you don't want to stay in your body," the owl says, preening her feathers. "Especially if you won't chew."

I dream of leaving my body, just like all the great novelists do. It's said that Pierre Menard, before writing *Don Quixote*, had been away from his body for so long spiders had spun webs in his ears.

"Your novel is waiting for you," my owl tells me. "It's so beautiful; it shivers with moonlight. You just need to eat more mice."

All I have to do is eat more mice, and get out of my body. Follow my owl. Return with my novel.

"And not get shot," says my owl.

It shouldn't still be hurting, but it does. A tiny, unhealed wound, my novel scampering off in the woods.

The intern looks up from his monitor. "The doctor will see you now."

THE ZOMBIE CURE

If you take the zombie cure, and you're not a zombie, then you'll turn into a zombie, but the other zombies will shun you.

If you are a zombie and you take the zombie cure, then you'll be cured, but you'll suffer side effects. You will become part of the insect kingdom. A leafcutter will land on your ear, she'll talk and you'll understand her. You'll go on with your life, but you'll have to take breaks to chew leaves, it'll be like a second job but you won't mind.

The other zombies will go on without you, forming their own zombie families; you'll see the pictures of their zombie children in your newsfeed while you chew and chew and chew. Every day you place a small green brick outside your house; the insect world flourishes around you once more.

You're learning how to hear music again; the insects teach you. Slowly you'll heal, you'll wander with purpose again.

HORSE

I hate grading papers so I go to the horse store and I buy a horse. I pick one with beautiful eyes and a demeanor of certainty, a horse who knows what is what in this world.

"Do you want to buy a bridle or a saddle to go with your new horse?" the salesman asks me.

"Oh no," I say. "I have too much grading I have to do, I'll never have time to ride."

I walk home with my horse, up three flights of stairs to my shitty apartment. My roommates look at me and my horse.

"That better be a rental," one of them says.

"Of course it's a rental," I say. "With all this grading I have to do, who has time to buy a horse?"

I push the horse into my tiny room, the floor covered in papers I'm supposed to grade, and pens.

I look my horse in the eye. "Please," I say. "Just help me get through this pile."

The horse looks at me stoically. "Only if I get to sing while I'm working," he says.

"Sing whatever you like," I say, relieved that the price of a horse's labor is so low these days.

The horse starts to sing, the same Taylor Swift song over and over, the one about the bleachers and t-shirts. It is the most awful thing I have ever heard, but the horse is making progress, dispersing grades and stamping out comments and corrections in the margins.

Before long the roommates are banging on the door.

"No," I yell at them. "Not until he's finished with my grading!"

"He's doing your grading?" they ask.

"Get your own goddamn horse," I say.

KISSING

1.

My kisses are so sweet you have to bolus for me every time, and I'm such a sloppy kisser, my beard tickles your face. So I've become such a delicate kisser, you say "Come on baby: don't hold back!"

And I'm such a serious kisser, my kisses solve all sorts of problems, but I'm such a playful kisser I get in trouble too.

I'm such a natural kisser you'd never know I spent thirty years in graduate school. I'm such a great kisser all those academic kissers should just go back to using their mouths for dissertations.

I'm such a sly kisser we've been lovers for decades and your mother thinks we're just friends.

2.

There are two kinds of kissers. There's the polite little peckers, the kind of people who only open their mouths to eat and talk and yawn, otherwise they're more concerned with gesture, the symbol instead of the thing itself.

They struggle with their kisses and they always win. Weak huggers, you have to do all the work and they come to resent it when you do.

They kiss like they're doing you a favor. They kiss like they care more about preventing the passage of germs. They kiss like they're gargling something more important than you.

I'm not one of those. Hugh Behm-Steinberg is a tongue man.

DICTIONARY

The first time you look up the word dictionary in the dictionary, it isn't there. There's dictionally, and there's dictograph, but no dictionary. You close the dictionary, examine the title. It's not a great dictionary, it's obsolete in many ways, but the pages, thin and soft, are one of your pleasures. It's the one you've held onto since you were a kid. The word should be in there (it's on the cover after all), but it's not.

So you open it once more, deliberately work your way through the D's, and where you should find the word dictionary, you find another dictionary, not the picture of a dictionary but an actual dictionary, the thing itself. It's so tiny, but you grab your magnifying glass and your tweezers. You wonder how much recursivity you're going to get. Is what lies open on your desk a dictionary of dictionaries of dictionaries, never exactly defining what the word means, only endlessly pointing at ever diminishing versions of itself?

You examine the little dictionary carefully, turning each delicate page with the tweezers, holding the magnifying glass steady with your other hand so the words stay in focus. But the little dictionary has no definitions, only the word *dictionary*, over and over, page after page, without pause or exceptions.

You close the little dictionary, then the big dictionary too, and put it back in its place on the shelf.

You wonder, when someone finally opens your book, and they ask who you are, whether you'll be able to say anything other than your own name, over and over again.

ALCHEMY

Trapped in that sort of alchemy where joy turns into anger, I go see another alchemist. She buys me chocolate milk, makes me sing. I don't feel like singing, she makes me sing, she harmonizes around me. I stop; she kicks my shin. "Don't stop," she says. I start over and after awhile I'm not alone, or don't feel so alone.

It was like that one time, when I was high with friends, I was watching a bike rodeo, because that was where my head was pointed, and I got so angry because it was so fake: everyone was just fucking around, everyone who was there. The best they could do was fuck around and my friends said, "It's just a rodeo, and what's so wrong with fucking around?" Stubborn experience.

My alchemist knows. Mostly I want to be serious, but my alchemist crosses me out and makes me eat a photograph of myself smiling. I look ridiculous so I start smiling. She says, "Can you feel it? Is it starting to work?"

"There's this image in your mind. It's photography's mother. It's how your mind creates the world; it's developing all the time," my alchemist says. "I know another way," she says.

I'm sweating light. My blood is light so mostly I spin. And spinning my light floods the room.

FIRE

My cat eats fire; when he is hungry he breathes it in and his fur reddens. I light a candle; he nibbles down the wick. I turn on the stove and he bats the kettle aside to gnaw on the burner. The furnace is always out, so the house gets cold, so cold all the mice huddle together in a ball for warmth by my pillow. Whimpering, they shiver so much that in my dreams I have to live in a house with no walls, only wind and so many cats breathing fire for company. I'm always off-balanced in these dreams, falling over as I keep having to tear off mouse-sized pieces of the house just to feed them.

In my dreams I am always that way. Sometimes the mice are made of fire, sometimes they're not, always I keep the cat away, never do the mice thank me. No pile of seeds, no bits of jewelry that only mice can find, not a song only they know how to sing will they ever sing for me.

I wake up and grab a bag of charcoal. I let the cat out and walk over to the barbecue; he gambols around like a kitten he is so happy. I pour the charcoal into the chimney and I set it alight. The cat mews, I keep telling him to wait. Soon it is roaring, soon it subsides, with a whoosh I pull the chimney up and the burning charcoal tumbles out grey and red and glowing. I put half the grate on, and some sausages on top of that for myself. With tongs now and then I grab a briquette and toss it across the pavement. My cat chases each one down, bats it a few times, then devours it quickly before it get a chance to cool.

I go inside to eat breakfast while my cat curls up and sleeps; the mice make their own plans. In ones and twos with tiny sparks in their mouths they leave. "We mean it this time," the note they leave behind says. It begins to snow.

That's ok, they always come back.

THE DEAD SEA

We go to the Dead Sea and then we go to the Dead Sea gift shop. After we go to the Dead Sea gift shop we go to the Dead Sea café. We eat salads because we're trying to eat healthy as we watch the Dead Sea ripple. We watch the Dead Sea traffic crawl by, we watch the Dead Sea army muster in the parking lot. Above us the Dead Sea airforce, below us who knows how much of our information twirls in the Dead Sea data farm.

You ask me, "How long do you have to stay in the Dead Sea until you die?"

"No one dies in the Dead Sea," I say.

So you ask me, "How long do you have to stay in the Dead Sea until you turn into a zombie?"

"I don't think it makes a difference," I say, my words dangling in the Dead Sea air, "whether you stay in the Dead Sea or not. How do you know we're not already zombies, that we've always been zombies?"

"I'm not a zombie. Do zombies eat salads?" you say, gesturing with your Dead Sea fork full of Dead Sea lettuce.

"We don't eat salads all the time," I say. The Dead Sea navy fire their guns.

"I'm going to eat a salad every day," you say. Maybe someone important is being buried.

"No, you won't." I say.

We drive away but the Dead Sea is all over us, we can feel it, we're helping it spread. We're never getting our deposit back.

EELS

One of the many nuisances in my life is that I have an eel that lives inside me. Its head sits in the cave of my mouth, and its body extends down my throat, through my stomach and into my guts. It likes me, it won't leave.

Whenever I'm near a bird it reaches out to eat it, and it won't let me have any no matter how nicely I ask.

Why do I put up with this? Why am I not living in the woods? Why do I let eel after eel bruise me this way?

I'm going to move to Japan. I will train with unagi masters. I will be marvelous. They will know what to do with me.

Or else I'm going to stick my cellphone charger in the eel's mouth. I want something out of this relationship, too.

ALONE TIME

For my birthday my wife got me a bug detector, so for kicks we went around the house looking for bugs. They were everywhere, of course, it's a surveillance society after all, but I was disappointed to find one inside our dryer.

"Maybe it's just there to tell the other appliances about our clothes," my wife said, but the bug detector said no, it was a deep official bug. This disappointed us because we loved climbing inside the dryer just to get away from it all, and now we knew they knew.

We stared at the bug in the dryer. Would we have to go back to passing notes back and forth? Then I thought what sort of data could it possibly get if the dryer was running? The bug most likely turned itself off when the dryer was turned on. So we called our kid and gave him instructions: set it for slow, NO HEAT, thirty minute timer, press the start button.

We climbed inside. Our kid shut the door and we started to tumble. It was dizzying, like the real world, but while it lasted we told and re-told each other all our secrets; we had many, many, many revolutionary ideas.

DEATH

In the beginning, there was Death; Death was really into video games. Because Death had all the time in the world, Death got really, really good at video games.

Death would say to God, "I'm bored," and God would say, "Well, have you played *Frogger* yet?" Death would say, "Ages ago! I know all the cheat codes!"

"Well, what about *Halo*?" God would say, and Death would say, "Yep, all versions too."

Death kept saying, "I'm so bored," and God would keep saying, "I'm busy, why don't you play more videogames?"

So, finally, Death says, "I've played them all, maybe I'll just go and make trouble."

That's when God says, "Wait a minute," and God shows Death the universe.

It takes forever to play. It keeps Death busy.

BEING BORN, BEING CARRIED

Sometimes you're born and you don't realize you've been born. You don't want to go anywhere but you go; you get carried.

You think you're so heavy but you're really light, you get carried all over the place. You say you don't like it, being born, being carried, but secretly it delights you. So you choose to get born, over and over again. "Here," everyone says, "let me show you."

You see the same faces you've seen countless times. Countless times, and yet it still delights you.

ANALYSIS

When the dollar collapses, new currencies will be made backed by wakefulness and sleep. The money of wakefulness will be generated by work and people acting like tigers; the tension generated by ferocity, of caging us and putting others in cages. The money of sleep must be spent at once, everything you make goes away when you wake up.

The currencies of wakefulness and sleep move together and separate on the commodities exchanges like dragonflies mating. Your brother corners the market on wakefulness, driving down the value of sleep. My sister says why bother investing in mattress makers? People will fall asleep anywhere.

Later, in separate warehouses, trucks depart with their containers, driving slowly east to pour everything we made into the sea.

Because I am old, I row towards these new reefs, hoping I'll find what was taken from me.

GOOD LUCK

Getting wacked with a cane by an old lady is good luck, the same as a bird shitting on your head. So my grandma goes into the city, she rides the bus. She meets the other old ladies and they ask "Have you dispensed any luck today?" and she says, "No, have you?" and they say, "No, me neither."

Mildred asks, "Why is it that if we can bring good luck into the world we don't?"

My grandma says, "Good luck is not the same as good: it doesn't make someone good it just makes them lucky. When a person thinks he's lucky he thinks he can be a jerk and get away with it, he can park in the handicapped parking spot and walk away without getting a ticket, or hang out with his no good friends and not suffer the consequences. Good luck is the opposite of good, and no one deserves it."

"I just wish," Mildred says, "I could beat someone with my cane who deserves it, and they'd get to be good instead of lucky."

My grandma stares at Mildred and says, "Don't you dare touch me with that cane of yours."

"You know what I mean," she says.

ALL MY TWINS

I talk too much; I boss the empty air, but doing this doesn't make me happy. So I set free the air – it brings me snakes; we converse as sisters.

So my twin brains me, and feeds my body to the sky, thinking it will bless her. The snakes coil at her feet, the snakes coil around her arms. Everyone cries, "What beautiful jewelry you wear!" Everyone loves her.

The sky blesses her; she twins, over and over, talking and talking and talking. The air is humid with chatter.

The air says, "Enough! I'm leaving California. I'm going to circulate over the Pacific Ocean for awhile and mind my own Etsy shop. All you copies can think about what you've done."

The twins invest in scuba gear and continue their conversations using tablets and dry erase markers. They pretend they're underwater, it's easier that way.

I come back from the sky with a headache and all my twins embrace me. Everyone breathes again, we have so much to say to one another. When our friends look for us, all they see are trees.

NATURE

You break up with Death and start dating Nature.

Nature is great. Nature knows all about long walks in the woods, and because Nature really likes you, all the rarest birds and animals come out to see you. They say the Mangarevan whistler is extinct but you've met three of them, heard their lovely whistles and that was just the second date!

On your third date Nature teaches all the coyotes how to howl one of your poems. Under the stars in the arms of Nature you hear the breath of the world.

And no kidding but Nature really, really, really, REALLLY loves sex. Nature has a problem with birth control, but what nature doesn't know won't hurt it.

Nature pulls you from your car and gets you walking everywhere. When you're tired Nature summons elephants to carry you wherever you wish to go. You look at your house and wonder why you need one. You're thinking of taking a sledgehammer to all the concrete around you. You see insects everywhere, all of them are chirping, "Go for it! Let Nature take care of everything!" All the pigeons say the same thing, and the fennel too.

You tell Nature you need some space, but rather than being hurt Nature brings you to the wilderness. You say, "No, that's not the space I mean," and Nature reluctantly brings you home to the city. You want to fight it out, clear the air, but Nature just agrees to everything, and when you back Nature into a corner all you get are mice, roaches and feral makeup sex.

"Why aren't you pregnant yet?" Nature keeps asking; you keep making excuses.

Finally, you say, "I think we should see other people," wondering if Nature will sulk like all your other ex's.

Nature says, "I'm way ahead of you."

"What do you mean?" you say.

"I'm seeing everybody already," Nature says. "I just want you to be who you already are."

"Call me when you want to hook up again," says Nature, that bringer of all gifts.

ON BEING A TEENAGER

1.

When I was a teenager my hair was a forest. It stretched for miles, and I could hardly go anywhere because someone was always tugging, or tying me up around trees or family or telephone poles. I tore so much of it out, thinking if it was so endless I could get away with wasting it. If I had had me some lovers I would have let them braid it for me, but I didn't so I stayed wild, and wore it loose with bangs that hid me about as well as I could hide my feelings.

When I was a teenager everyone wore their hair like that. No one was going anywhere, and if they had lovers they treated them awkwardly. I wasn't good at getting out of my body, even when I shaved all of it off.

2.

My counselor refused to let me drop biology class, no matter how often I told her I hated it. "You need to get used to bodies," she said. "I know you don't want to but you do."

So I signed up for theatre classes. What I loved best were the warm up exercises. I loved tensing and relaxing the different parts of me, rolling my shoulders, becoming rubbery. We'd sit in the darkened auditorium while the teacher taught us how to cry. We'd sit there with our eyes closed, thinking our saddest thoughts, but I just couldn't. All I felt were my shoulders cramping, as if I'd been carrying something so heavy I'd never be allowed to know what it was.

3.

When I turned into a teenager, one of the things I grew to hate were chin-ups. To hang off a bar and yank my body up, over and over, only to fall back down again mindlessly; there were just so many better things I could do. The gym coach would lash out at me and my laziness.

"What if," he said, "there was a terrible accident, and you were dangling from a cliff, and the only thing saving you from certain death was the strength of your wrists, would you not at that moment regret blowing off all those chin-ups in gym class?"

"Fuck no," I said. "I have a backup plan. Why do you think I've been masturbating so furiously all these years?"

IN WHICH I GET A JOB AS A POWER TROWEL REPLACEMENT

My legs are so unemployed they rattle when I walk, so the employment office calls. It doesn't matter that I'm busy thinking, that I've got this novel I'm working on. "We're cutting you off," they say. "You can think on someone else's time."

I'm put to work smoothing cement. Instead of being handed a machine, the robots pick me up and put me down in harness; in between I dance nonstop. There's a lot of us doing this; there's so many trip hazards in this world.

If I think about it it's terrifying, because everything's so smooth now, and instead of working on my novel I'm stuck wondering how this all came to be. All the people that must be needed to make everything smooth, all the novels it cost – no one encountering obstacles as they in turn are picked up and put down to go to work.

At the end of each day they let us go and we wobble. The lucky among us moonlight as jackhammers, carving great books on the terrible flatness of this city.

ORIGIN STORY

One day I go to the dentist; I'm in the chair, the assistant is poking around. I need a deep cleaning, and because I have good insurance, I get the nitrous.

The assistant says uh-oh, and the dentist is brought in. The amount of work that needs to be done is substantial, urgent and extremely painful. I regret my diet of gravel and generic soda.

They knock me out.

When I come to everyone is smiling, and my face feels like it doesn't belong to me. "Mr. Glockenspiel," the dentist says, "The damage was severe; almost everything had to go. We had to take extraordinary measures just to save your life. The good news: we gave you a beak!"

They hand me a mirror, and it's true, I now have a beak. Yellow, but realistic, with white under-shadings, and curving slightly downward. I try to smile but out comes a piercing cry.

I look surprisingly powerful, like I could tear someone's throat out, if I wanted to. All the people waiting, the dentists and their assistants and billing specialists smile at me as I walk out, and when they do I cry back, louder each time.

I'm only partially a bird, but already my thoughts are taking flight. I no longer have to live my old life handing out parking tickets, collecting stamps and ignoring the injustice that surrounds me.

I'm going to live in the mountains! I'm going to seek out forgotten gods and they will bestow upon me superpowers and symbols of strength, endurance and mystery. I'm going to study justice and the Geneva Convention. I'm going to acquire wings.

I'll never have to floss again.

THE MAYORS

The mayors go for a walk, and your mom walks along with them, and she takes you with her, so you're walking with the mayors too.

You start in town and walk into the city. You're told all the cities are moaning; you ask your mom, "Why are they moaning?" She says they want to be wild places again, if you listen carefully that's what they're saying.

When you stop for the ribbon-cutting ceremony, you lay your head on the sidewalk and your mom protects you from all the people; you're listening very carefully, and all the mayors think that's sweet.

Who will you be, what will you do, when your mom's no longer there, only the ocean, and aldermen?

MY HEART

You shyly steal my heart. You swap it with a sleeping raccoon. I wash my hands all the time. I'm not afraid of anything.

When you turn on the light, I get up on my legs; I put my hands on your door. I'm loud, I keep you up.

You say to me, "C'mon."

And I say to you, "No, you c'mon."

"Let me in," I say.

I hang out with the other raccoons. They're nice, but they're not you. None of them have my heart.

BEARS

A bear is a gesture, the gesture of touching, which is to pull. The bear can't stop talking; he keeps secrets by telling them. Telling somebody a secret is delicious: it's to be covered in fur and growl all the time.

Your children, their wet fur, their playing are patterns which break and rebuild, rise up and get kicked over. It's reactive in a way they can't articulate, they repeat and the repetitions are magic; the children do magic and they understand all the animals. It's a method of touching, very lightly, so that their parents turn back from far away, wherever that is.

Your children asking you who are you going to be, and you look as far away as you can, and you say, "There, that's who I'm going to be."

"Oh," they say. "We've been there already; it's kind of boring, but okay."

"Smell this," they say.

JOB INTERVIEW

Why act responsibly? Post all my browser history, the images of me smoking dope with the Secretary of the Interior.

"He needs it," I told everyone at the interview, "because he's so fucking shy. He thinks all his crimes are secrets."

Don't you remember, at the press conference, when he declared that, as the Secretary of the Interior, he had a right to know what everyone was thinking? "The interior includes everything that's inside," he said. "That means what you keep in your heart," pointing to the reporter from *The Washington Post*.

Nobody remembers what gets said at press conferences. It's why we keep having press conferences, so more people can forget what was once said.

The Secretary of the Interior could care less about what's going on outside. "That's the job of the Secretary of the Exterior," he said. After he passed me the roach, I told him we don't have a Secretary of the Exterior. "That's how much the outside matters," he said. "Maybe you should apply for the job."

ASCETIC ACID

The effects are disappointing; you get some hallucinations but they're always restrained. You remember that you're naturally transparent, that if you just relaxed in your trip you could be fully invisible.

"Nothing is worth seeing anyway," says the drug, and because it's inside you you find it very convincing.

When you come down, you're naked and you've given away all your possessions, weeping with joy. You feel light and happy to feel that way. The hangover lasts for years.

DEATH #2

It stinks; every day you have to walk by the house where Death lives. Death sleeps in, smokes too much. Everyone knows it's the party house. You exhale when you walk by.

Death opens the curtains, looks out, sees you. Death keeps wanting to date again, but instead of working on his OK Cupid profile, he keeps calling you. "I miss you!" he yells as you walk by.

You put Death off. "I'm too busy for this," you tell him. "I'm seeing someone else."

"Who?" Death asks.

"I'm not going to tell you, and you know why."

It stinks that every house you walk by smells like Death. You think maybe you should cut back on your own smoking. "Quit calling me," you say.

Death says, "Fine, I hope both of you live forever!"

He doesn't mean it, but you wonder how long it will take for him to figure that out.

YO-YO

I go to the eyeball store. I tell the owner I'm just looking, and she says, "No, you're not, not really, you're just being hesitant. You want a third eye."

I say, "You're right, I've been shopping for one for some time now; I believe I'm ready."

The owner asks me if I have my papers, so I show her the note from my spiritual advisor. She says that's nice, but when I show her my Orange Belt Certificate, which represents the growing power of the sun, how I'm beginning to feel my body and mind open and develop, she sits me down, she puts her hand on my head.

"Forward or back?" she asks.

Then time, I meet time, she's using the universe as her personal yo-yo, she's showing me her tricks. She makes it look so easy; she's going around the world, she's walking the dog, she's rocking the baby.

Later the owner shows me my eye. I open and close it very deliberately at first, but soon I don't have to think, I just choose and I see. As soon as I get my x-ray monocle, I am going to have a magnificent life.

FROGS

The frogs bully you. They stick their tongues out, they sneak up and rub their mucus into you; worse, you wake up with tadpoles.

The frogs say, "Trust us, we'll be back soon."

The tadpoles thrash around. You feel terrible—they're just babies, innocent, none of this is their fault.

So you slide them into your sink. You raise the stopper, fill it up with water; they circle and calm. You decide to take raising them seriously. You get an aquarium, tadpole food (mosquito larvae), an aerator that looks like a pirate chest. Their parents are assholes, but you will raise their children for them.

And even though the support checks never come, even though you hear nothing on their birthdays, you raise them as your own; you don't say anything bad to them about their birthparents. You learn how to sing like a frog so you can sing properly to them, so they won't grow up to be lonely.

The frogs act serious when they see you, but you know they're just fucking with you, because they're jerks. You keep waking up with more tadpoles in your bed, the cycle of life continues, until they stop seeing you, which means time passes, and the adults have found someone else to pick on.

Some of the tadpoles grow to love you; others get into trouble. One day all of them, now full grown frogs, come to you. "We have to leave," they say.

"But it's dangerous out there!" you say, obviously worried. "The toxic waste, the herons with their beaks, gourmet chefs!"

"We'll be okay—you did great," they say. "Don't blame yourself for anything that happens to us." Then they're gone, and your house slowly fills up with mosquitos once more.

But later, when you go walking through your favorite swamp, you hear your name amidst the chirping. You don't recognize the voice as that of any of the frogs you raised, so you're curious and walk deeper into the swamp.

They're not really singing to you, they're just singing to each other. A lot of frogs, all singing, and every so often there's your name. You wish you had taken the time to get better at understanding the language of frogs, but it still delights you to find out your name has become a note in their song.

Unlike what they say about you, all those mosquitos you also raised.

THE SOUND OF THE WAR

Distractions everywhere but we still hear the sound of the war. Those who can afford them wear war-canceling earbuds; the rest of us suffer.

The worst is when we hear someone we know in the war, we're talking to them and we're here, but they're in the war. "Why are you flinching like that?" they ask, and we apologize and say, "It's nothing."

They look at us like we don't know what we're talking about. We don't know what we're talking about. We're just trying our best to stop listening to the war.

THE LAND

We swim because we're swimmers. We need a pool, but all the pools are filled with people. They thrash around trying to swim. They keep bumping into each other and fighting. The water's so cold they shiver. Every pool we go to it's the same. The lakes, rivers and oceans, all the same: crowded, cold, fighting. All that, and the land which hates us, that reminds us with every step we don't belong here.

"I don't want to freeze," I say.

"Come on in," you say. "You're not afraid of suffering, are you?"

CROWNS

I keep thinking about crowns, the idea that we are all promised one, or that no one, not even kings, wears them anymore. Aren't they the least comfortable of hats? Aren't they useless when it is snowing, or even dangerous when there's lightning? When you get one, would you insist on wearing yours or would you keep it on your vanity? Would you hang out with those who wore theirs or would you trade it in for something you weren't able to bring with you? Maybe the sun is a crown because no one can wear it.

Patchy fog by the river. A stranger accompanies you, he hands you yours and you hold it, wondering whether it's supposed to feel like it does.

Will you look for me, will you still recognize me when I'm wearing mine?

SLEEP

My wife sleeps, I stay up. I go to sleep, she wakes up and wakes me too. "I've been having these amazing dreams!" she cries. She describes them intricately, and they always have pirates.

But I'm already falling asleep; I'm on a ship, full of treasure, rocking slowly back and forth on the sea.

BILLABLE HOURS

The father you should have had becomes your lawyer. You commit more crimes, complicate your transactions, just to spend more time with him. When you call him with your one-and-only phone call, he'll tell you they kept supper in the oven for you, and that he loves you and he knows you're going to make it. When you go to the playground, you wish his office was nearby, and that, ignoring an important client, he would stare out the window just to watch you selling pot by the swings.

YOUR WHALE

Your whale calls. It's been three weeks. You have to take your children back. Your whale wants to do other things with its time.

Your children don't like staying in your house. There's too much land there. You take them to the pool so they'll be happy, but they never want to get out of the pool.

You should be more firm, but you love watching them swim. They remind you of your whale.

THINGS

The older children are nervous about the newer children. When we take them to the nursery, they sob louder than the babies.

"There are so many of them," they cry. "How much love will you have left for us?"

We look around in our bags, pull out toys and makeup and tissues and car keys, and they say, "Things? Things! You think we're going to mistake shoddy materialisms for love?"

And the babies say to their brothers and sisters, "In time, eventually, you will."

A kid tugs at my arm, she says, "You better be carrying a puppy in that bag of yours."

EELS #2

I met Lorraine at the support group. We both knew you're not supposed to date someone you meet at your support group, because it's not really love you're feeling when you hook up, it's the release of being with someone who has the same problems as you.

Still, I thought, it would be so nice to go out with someone and not have to explain why there was an eel inside my mouth nipping at her when we're trying to kiss.

We kept having sex because we kept running out of things to say, but at least our eels got along. We let them loose in her bathtub and watched them thrash in the water. I got so frustrated—why couldn't we just be like our eels, satisfied with twining around each other all the time?

What was worse was when my eel left me for her eel; I couldn't look at Lorraine, and she wouldn't understand why. "It's part of their life cycle; it's nothing personal," she said. "We should still see each other," she said.

Lorraine kept wanting to know if I was willing at least to carry some of the eggs, to go with her to the Sargasso sea, but without an eel of my own what kind of man was I?

So I went to stand in the cold river, my mouth open for anyone who wanted me, wondering if any eel would take me seriously again for giving my heart away so freely.

THE WOODS

Until it's over, we will live in the woods. We will avoid all roads and what paths there are we will obscure them, the better to hide ourselves. Each morning, I will set out with my wife and the deer. We will go out for drinks together. I will keep a tab, and the bartender will call me "The Zipper." When the hunters come, maybe the bartender will hide us, maybe the bartender will lead the hunters to wherever we're hiding. We're never sure we've obscured our paths well enough.

We keep drinking when we can; we pay when we can to keep the bartender happy. We're never sure if we've been keeping our bartender happy enough. Sometimes he lets something slip, and when we walk back into the woods we swear never to go back. We stay in the woods until we can't stand it, terrified each time a twig snaps, or one of the deer we love goes missing.

We go back, each time taking a different route. We slide into our stools, the news is never on, but we can guess by the commercials, how happy the actors look to drive in cars, eat at restaurants, drink soda pop. The bartender says we should relax, everything's fine, everything's exactly the way it's supposed to be. The deer chortle when they hear that. We can't afford to get drunk, still, we stagger out when the bar closes, we walk in the dark through the woods, to wherever we're staying as we hide in the woods.

THE SHARING ECONOMY

In future homes across America each will have its own jail cell built right in. That way every homeowner can make a little extra cash. All of us will become accustomed to being wardens, all of us will sometimes be prisoners, too. Our children will grow used to befriending people they're not supposed to see.

It'll be like owning a friend, a prisoner talking to us as we eat dinner, a prisoner watching football when we're watching football. They'll fold our laundry; they'll visit with us while we're on parole.

ON THE POST-APOCALYPTIC

I'm working on a novel about this guy wandering through a post-apocalyptic landscape having various adventures that don't lead anywhere. He just keeps moving, somewhere or anywhere. Then he meets another person and that person is reading a novel about this guy who's wandering through a post-apocalyptic landscape, having various adventures, not getting anywhere, etc.

"Am I the same guy?" he thinks, so he borrows the book, and the novel I'm writing gets written by someone else, leaving me time to catch up on various household chores.

I'm okay with this happening. I like this world.

PAPAYA

A little dirt is always coming out of my ears. I joke with my friends and attribute it to all the time I spend with my head underground, hiding from the news of the world.

But I'm fertile, as much as I was when I was a child, when my mother, that eater of papayas, wedged seeds down my ears. I learned to live with my head held up to receive maximum sunlight, to let the bees do their work, but I had to run away from home, and some nights I still wake up with her on top of me, demanding her share of the fruit.

"How are you able to function?" the doctors all cry, and I explain my deftness with metaphors and workarounds. Long ago I diversified and rotated what I thought about. I now achieve a complex sweetness in what I do. I work all the farmers' markets and have my own line of baby food.

I talk to you about love, I do it every day. I'd do it even if nothing green grew inside me. I'd do it even if nobody paid me for anything.

There's an orchard inside me, I protect it with my life. You don't know what a mother is capable of. There's a tree inside my head, and I am always hiding you behind it, just in case.

KRISHNA

So one day I steal the flute, the one He plays and everyone loves him. I take it home and show it to my wife. She says, "Are you nuts, what do you want an enchanted flute for? You don't even know how to play the flute."

And it was true, when I tried to play I was awful and everyone hated me. "Go to the shed and practice," my wife says. "Maybe you'll learn how to play the bloody thing." At this point it was starting to drip.

I go to live in the shed, and all day and all night I practice. When I'm not watching magic flute instruction videos on my cell phone I practice. All the time, for weeks and months, my beard grows down to my stomach.

Later I know I'm getting good when the ants change their formation to listen to me, and the squirrels shyly leave me pieces of fruit. Finally my wife leads me back into the house, and I play my best for her. She shaves my beard, cuts my hair and makes love to me.

Afterwards she says, "I would have done that anyway," and "Oh, by the way, while you've been practicing in the shed, He's been over here, crashing on our couch. He's been doing light errands around the house and listening to you practice on His flute."

"Is he still here?" I ask.

"He's probably in the kitchen eating a grilled Elvis."

So barefoot, naked even, holding my flute, it's my house after all, I go downstairs. And I look at Him; He looks at me. Of course He has another flute, and together we play, and as we play a rightness comes over the world. One that cannot last, but is good while it does.

PARADE

I'm a horse, just wandering around the neighborhood. It's very nice out; I decide I'll visit the preschool where I had so many fond memories from when I was a foal. I leap the fence, and I'm surrounded by toddlers in awe of me. Of course, I'm a horse, enormous and calm; I let them pet me. I'll be their secret, I breathe deeply as only a horse can, and the children are so happy.

Later the day turns toward naptime, I go inside to lie down. Mrs. Sanchez whispers in my ear that perhaps I'm a little big for preschool, but my eyes are soft and pleading. I tell her I'm not going to stay forever, I just want to be nostalgic for a short time longer. I'm a horse: it is my right.

One of the bigger kids feeds me carrots she stole from the snack room. I am somber; she doesn't yet understand what she is doing. I kneel down very carefully and let her mount me. When she is older she'll imagine we galloped, and while we did this her life divided, but I walk very carefully, the other children trailing behind us. We are a parade.

YOUR SEWING SKILLS

I wake up and you tell me to hold still; we're still in surgery and you haven't finished sewing me up. I sigh, close my eyes and try to go back to sleep while in the furthest away part of my body I feel your needle neatly stitching me.

I wake up again and you're still working, I go back to sleep and wake up again, you're still working. "You have no idea how much sewing up you need every night," you say. "All those assholes at work and their claws," you say.

Every day I go back to work a little tender. I like to think it makes me so good at my job.

I should quit, but I won't, I'll never.

As much as I like my work, I love how jealous all my coworkers get when they see the magnificence of your stitchery.

CLASSROOM GUIDE

One of the questions around *Animal Children* is, "What sort of book is this? Is it poetry? Fiction? Something else?" So a good jumping off point might be to examine the idea of genre, starting with asking the class how they know something is a poem? How do they know something is a story?

One way to approach this is to try to create definitions or rules or a formula: for example, if a text rhymes, it's a poem. What are the pros and cons of that approach? Another way is to imagine genre as a field (a big circle on the chalkboard), where the closer to the center you get, the more everyone agrees that what we have is a poem, and the closer we get to the edge, well that's where the weirdness starts and we start to argue. Why might a writer want to be in the middle of a genre field? Why might a writer want to be on the edge? Then pull back: What purpose do genre labels like poetry and fiction serve for readers and writers? How might they shape our expectations before we even begin reading? How might they even form communities?

Because *Animal Children* has one foot in poetry and the other in prose, it makes a great transitional work in a creative writing class, as students move from trying their hands at poetry and turn to writing prose (or vice versa). What happens when stories become very short? What else is going on in these pieces besides telling stories?

WRITING EXERCISE

Write down a sentence that describes a dilemma: a problem to be solved or an obstacle to be overcome. Pass this to your right. With the dilemma/problem/obstacle, write another sentence that responds, but in a weird, indirect way that makes things worse. Pass it along to the right. Write another sentence, this time putting in some context or scenery or character building—whatever you like; but ideally you want to go sideways somehow, rather than making more trouble for our protagonists. One more time, pass it to your right. With what's in front of you, write three-to-five more sentences and finish the story, so long as you don't let your protagonist off the hook.

ACKNOWLEDGEMENTS

Every book is the work of a community, and *Animal Children* would not be possible without the support, advice, care, and advocacy of so many people.

I would like to thank Katie Farris and the NaSSSWriMo group, where many of these narratives first came to life.

I'd also like to thank Colleen Mckee, Elise Hunter, Tim Xonnelly, Paul Corman-Roberts, Giavanna Ortiz de Candia, and the other members of the Au Coquelet writing group, whose feedback was invaluable.

A shout out to Sarah Kobrinsky for the use of her floor and her editorial eye, transforming what seemed like just a bunch of weird prose pieces into an actual book.

Deep and humble love to J. K. Fowler, Michaela Mullin, and all the people at Nomadic Press for adding me to their family. Gratitude to Arthur Johnstone for the beautiful cover.

Many, many thanks to Alisa Golden, Josh Wilson, Christopher James, Jason Teal, Joyce Jenkins and Richard Silberg, Evan Karp, Katie Riegel, Michael Mejia, and all the editors who first published these stories in their amazing journals and magazines.

But most of all, and always, my deepest love and joy to my wife Mary Behm-Steinberg and her patient stitchery.

Thank you to the following publications, where some of these pieces first appeared:

"Your Whale," "On the Post-Apocalyptic" and "Gentleness," *82 Review*
"Alchemy" and "Yo-yo," *45th Parallel*
"All My Twins," *Another Chicago Magazine*

"The Sharing Economy" (originally published as "Newest Industry"),
    Anvil Lit Review
"Krishna," *The Fabulist*
"4-H," *Gigantic*
"Origin Story," *Great Jones Street*
"The Zombie Cure," *Heavy Feather Review*
"Bears," "Dictionary," "Eels," "Eels #2," "Goodwill," "Horse" and "Parade,"
    Jellyfish Review
"Death," "Nature" and "Death #2," *Phoebe*
"Billable Hours" and "Things," *Poetry Flash*
"The Sea," *Poetry International*
"Soft Spot," "Kissing" and "On Being a Teenager," *sPARKLE and bLINK*
"In Which I Get a Job as a Power Trowel Replacement," *Sweet*
"Ascetic Acid," *Truck*
"Me and My Owl," *Western Humanities Review*

Recipient of a Wallace Stegner and NEA Creative Writing Fellowship, **HUGH BEHM-STEINBERG** is the author of two collections of poetry, *Shy Green Fields* (No Tell Books, 2007) and *The Opposite of Work* (JackLeg Press, 2012; 2nd edition by Doubleback Books, 2020). In 2015, his short story "Taylor Swift" won the Barthelme Prize for short fiction, and his story "Goodwill" was picked as one of Wigleaf's Top Fifty Very Short Fictions of 2018. He teaches writing and literature at California College of the Arts, where he is currently the Chief Steward of the Adjunct Faculty Union, SEIU 1021.